Harriet Beecher Stowe, Emily Weaver

Dialogues and scenes from the writings of Harriet Beecher

Stowe

Harriet Beecher Stowe, Emily Weaver

Dialogues and scenes from the writings of Harriet Beecher Stowe

ISBN/EAN: 9783337124571

Printed in Europe, USA, Canada, Australia, Japan

Cover: Foto ©Andreas Hilbeck / pixelio.de

More available books at **www.hansebooks.com**

The Riverside Literature Series

DIALOGUES AND SCENES

FROM THE WRITINGS OF

HARRIET BEECHER STOWE

ARRANGED BY

EMILY WEAVER

HOUGHTON, MIFFLIN AND COMPANY
Boston: 4 Park Street; New York: 11 East Seventeenth Street
The Riverside Press, Cambridge
1889

The Riverside Press, Cambridge:
Electrotyped and Printed by H. O. Houghton & Co.

PREFATORY NOTE.

THE use to which the following little work may be put is twofold. It offers to schools which desire to hold some special exhibition material for simple and easily effected dramatic representation; and it provides classes also with lively and spirited dialogue for reading exercises.

Great care has been taken to adhere to the original text as closely as possible; and in order to make the dialogue clear and to explain the action, explanatory passages from the book in which the dialogue occurs are added from time to time. They are distinguished from the parts to be acted by being printed in smaller type and enclosed in brackets [ ].

The costumes and properties for the scenes will not generally be found hard to procure, and a little ingenuity will often remove apparent difficulties. It is not the elaborate, but the simple and inexpensive setting of dramatic scenes which gives most pleasure on the school-stage.

It will often be found, however, that a spirited and attractive representation will be secured, simply by assigning the several parts to different pupils, and expecting them by their fidelity in reading the parts to convey to the school or audience the effect intended by the author to be produced. In this manner the dialogues will offer a pleasing change in reading exercises, and the readers will become familiar with the writing of one of the most eminent of American authors.

CONTENTS.

CHARACTERS.

Mr. Bird, the senator.

Mrs. Bird, a little, blue-eyed, rosy-cheeked woman.

Tom,
Jim, } children of Mr. and Mrs. Bird.
Mary,

Eliza, a good-looking quadroon (very nearly white), with black eyes and hair.

Harry, her son, a boy of between four and five years of age, with black hair and dark eyes.

Cudjoe, an old negro, servant to Mr. Bird.

Dinah, an old negress, servant to Mrs. Bird.

John van Trompe, a very big, sandy-haired, rough-looking man.

COSTUMES.

Mr. Bird. A dark-colored suit of clothes; a pair of worked slippers; spectacles; and in Scenes IV. and V. an overcoat and boots.

Mrs. Bird. A full-skirted black dress; hair parted in the middle, and arranged very low on the temples, and coiled or twisted at the back of the head.

Tom and Jim, in short trowsers and blouses fastened round the waist with a belt.

Mary, in short frock and white pinafore.

Eliza, in Scenes II. and III. in a torn dress, soiled and splashed, only one shoe, and torn stockings. In Scene IV. a neat dark dress, a shawl, and a bonnet.

Harry, "a gay robe of scarlet and yellow plaid, carefully made and neatly fitted."

Cudjoe and Dinah, neatly and plainly dressed. Dinah with apron.

John van Trompe must wear a red flannel shirt, and no collar or tie.

ANALYSIS OF SCENES: PROPERTIES.

SCENE I.   A parlor in Mr. Bird's house, with exit.   Mrs. Bird denounces the new law against helping escaped slaves, and announces her intention of breaking it as soon as she gets a chance Her husband defends the law, and says that he has voted for it.

PROPERTIES.   Chairs, table, rocking-chair, rug, and carpet suitable for parlor; cups and saucers, teapot, etc., camphor-bottle; newspaper; boots.   Pictures on the walls, and curtains.

SCENE II.   Kitchen in Mr. Bird's house, with exit.   Eliza begs Mrs. Bird to protect her, and the senator suggests that they should give her some clothes.

PROPERTIES.   Plain chairs and table, settle.   (Bright tins and dish-covers may be hung on the walls, or a shelf holding plates and dishes may be shown; in fact, any articles that will assist to give the idea of a kitchen will be appropriate to this scene.)

SCENE III.   Same as in Scene II.   Eliza gives an account of her escape.

PROPERTIES.   Same as in Scene II.

SCENE IV.   Same as in Scene I.   Mr. Bird decides to take Eliza to a place of safety.

PROPERTIES.   Same as in Scene I., omitting the teapot, cups and saucers.   Also a dress and some clothes for little boy; needle, scissors, thimble, etc.

SCENE V.   Kitchen in Van Trompe's house, with exit.   Mr. Bird puts Eliza under the protection of John van Trompe.

PROPERTIES.   Rough furniture; two or three rifles on the walls.   Two candles and candlesticks.   Ten-dollar bill.

SENATOR BIRD.

Scene I. *A parlor.*

[The light of the cheerful fire shines on the rug and carpet of a cosy parlor, and glitters on the sides of the teacups and well-brightened teapot, as Senator Bird is drawing off his boots, preparatory to inserting his feet in a pair of new handsome slippers, which his wife has been working for him while he was away on his senatorial tour. Mrs. Bird, looking the very picture of delight, superintends the arrangements of the table, ever and anon mingling admonitory remarks to a number of frolicsome juveniles, who are effervescing in all those modes of untold gambol and mischief that have astonished mothers ever since the Flood.]

Curtain rises on Mr. and Mrs. Bird and their children.

MRS. BIRD.

Tom, let the door-knob alone; there's a man! Mary, Mary! don't pull the cat's tail. Poor pussy! Jim, you mustn't climb on that table; no, no! You don't know, my dear [to her husband], what a surprise to us all to see you here to-night!

MR. BIRD.

Yes, yes, I thought I'd just make a run down, spend the night, and have a little comfort at home. I'm tired to death, and my head aches!

[Mrs. Bird casts a glance at a camphor-bottle which stands in the half - open closet, and appears to meditate an approach to it, but her husband interposes.]

No, no, Mary, no doctoring! A cup of your good hot tea and some of our good home living is what I want. It's a tiresome business, this legislating!

[And the senator smiles as if he rather liked the idea of considering himself a sacrifice to his country.]

MRS. BIRD.

Well, and what have they been doing in the Senate?

MR. BIRD.

[opening his eyes in surprise at the question.]

Not very much of importance.

MRS. BIRD.

Well; but is it true that they have been passing a law forbidding people to give meat and drink to those poor colored folks that come along? I heard they were talking of some such law, but I did n't think any Christian legislature would pass it!

MR. BIRD.

Why, Mary, you are getting to be a politician all at once.

MRS. BIRD.

No, nonsense! I would n't give a fig for all your politics generally, but I think this is something downright cruel and unchristian. I hope, my dear, no such law has been passed.

MR. BIRD.

There has been a law passed forbidding people to help off the slaves that come over from Kentucky, my dear. So much of that thing has been done by these reckless Abolitionists, that our brethren in Kentucky are very strongly excited, and it seems necessary, and no more than christian and kind, that something should be done by our State to quiet the excitement.

MRS. BIRD.

And what is the law? It does n't forbid us to shelter these poor creatures a night, does it; and to give 'em something comfortable to eat and a few old clothes, and to send them quietly about their business?

MR. BIRD.

Why, yes, my dear; that would be aiding and abetting, you know.

[Mrs. Bird is a timid, blushing little woman about four feet in height, with mild blue eyes and a peach-blow complexion, and the gentlest, sweetest voice in the world. . . . There is only one thing that is capable of arousing her, and that provocation comes in on the side of her unusually gentle and sympathetic nature : anything in the shape of cruelty will throw her into a passion which is the more alarming and inexplicable in proportion to the general softness of her nature. On the present occasion, Mrs. Bird rises quickly, with very red cheeks, which quite improve her general appearance, and walks up to her husband, with quite a resolute air, and speaks in a determined tone.]

MRS. BIRD.

Now, John, I want to know if you think such a law as that is right and Christian ?

MR. BIRD.

You won't shoot me, now, Mary, if I say I do !

MRS. BIRD.

I never could have thought it of you, John ; you did n't vote for it?

MR. BIRD.

Even so, my fair politician.

MRS. BIRD.

You ought to be ashamed, John ! Poor, homeless, houseless creatures ! It's a shameful, wicked, abominable law, and I 'll break it, for one, the first time I get a chance ; and I hope I shall have a chance, I do ! Things have got to a pretty pass, if a woman can't give a warm supper and a bed to poor starving creatures, just because they are slaves and have been abused and oppressed all their lives, poor things !

MR. BIRD.

But, Mary, just listen to me. Your feelings are all quite right, dear, and interesting, and I love you for them ; but then, dear, we must n't suffer our feelings to run away with our judgment ; you must consider it 's not a matter of private feeling, — there are great public interests involved : there is such a state of public agitation rising that we must put aside our private feelings.

MRS. BIRD.

Now, John, I don't know anything about politics, but I can read my Bible ; and there I see that I must feed the hungry, clothe the naked, and comfort the desolate ; and that Bible I mean to follow.

MR. BIRD.

But in cases where your doing so would involve a great public evil —

MRS. BIRD.

Obeying God never brings on public evils. I know it can't. It 's always safest, all round, to do as He bids us.

MR. BIRD.

Now listen to me, Mary, and I can state to you a very clear argument, to show —

MRS. BIRD.

Oh, nonsense, John ! you can talk all night, but you would n't do it. I put it to you, John : would *you* now turn away a poor, shivering, hungry creature from your door, because he was a runaway? *Would* you now?

[Now, if the truth must be told, our senator has the misfortune to be a man who has a particularly humane and accessible nature, and turning away anybody that is in trouble never has been his forte. So he has recourse to the usual means of gaining time for such cases made and provided; he says "ahem," and coughs several times, takes out his pocket-handkerchief, and begins to wipe his glasses.]

I should like to see you doing that, John, I really should! Turning a woman out of doors in a snow-storm, for instance; or, maybe you'd take her up and put her in jail, would n't you? You would make a great hand at that!

MR. BIRD.

[in a moderate tone.]

Of course, it would be a very painful duty.

MRS. BIRD.

Duty, John! don't use that word! You know it is n't a duty — it can't be a duty. If folks want to keep their slaves from running away, let 'em treat 'em well, — that 's my doctrine. If I had slaves (as I hope I never shall have), I 'd risk their wanting to run away from me, or you either, John. I tell you folks don't run away when they are happy; and when they do run, poor creatures! they suffer enough with cold and hunger and fear, without everybody turning against them; and, law or no law, I never will, so help me God!

Mary! Mary! My dear, let me reason with you.

MRS. BIRD.

I hate reasoning, John, — especially reasoning on such subjects. There's a way you political folks have of coming round and round a plain right thing; and you don't believe in it yourselves when it comes to practice. I know *you* well enough, John. You don't believe it's right any more than I do; and you would n't do it any sooner than I.

[At this critical juncture, old Cudjoe, the black man-of-all-work, puts his head in at the door.]

CUDJOE.

Missis, would you come into the kitchen?

[Our senator, tolerably relieved, looks after his little wife with a whimsical mixture of amusement and vexation, and seating himself in the arm-chair, begins to read the papers. After a moment, his wife's voice is heard at the door, in a quick, earnest tone.]

MRS. BIRD.

John! John! I do wish you'd come here a moment.

Curtain falls.

SCENE II. *A kitchen.*

[Mr. Bird lays down his paper and goes into the kitchen, and starts, quite amazed at the sight that presents itself : A young and slender woman, with garments torn and frozen, with one shoe gone, and the stocking torn away from the cut and bleeding foot, lies back in a deadly swoon upon two chairs. There is the impress of the despised race on her face, yet none can help feeling its mournful and pathetic beauty, while its stony sharpness, its cold, fixed, and deathly aspect, strikes a solemn chill over him. He draws his breath short, and stands in silence. His wife and their only colored domestic, old Aunt Dinah, are busily engaged in restorative measures ; while old Cudjoe has got the boy (Eliza's son) on his knee, and is busy pulling off his shoes and stockings and chafing his little cold feet.]

Curtain rises.

DINAH.
[compassionately.]

Sure, now, if she ain't a sight to behold!—'pears like 't was the heat that made her faint. She was tol'able peart when she cum in, and asked if she could n't warm herself here a spell ; and I was just a-askin' her where she cum from, and she fainted right down. Never done much hard work, guess, by the looks of her hands.

MRS. BIRD.

Poor creature !

[The woman slowly uncloses her large dark eyes, and looks vacantly at Mrs. Bird. Suddenly an expression of agony crosses her face and she springs up.]

ELIZA.

Oh, my Harry! Have they got him?

[The boy at this jumps from Cudjoe's knee, and running to her side, puts up his arms.]

Oh, he's here! he's here! Oh, ma'am! do protect us! don't let them get him.

MRS. BIRD.

[encouragingly.]

Nobody shall hurt you here, poor woman. You are safe; don't be afraid.

ELIZA.

God bless you!

[The woman covers her face, and sobs; while the boy, seeing her cry, tries to get into her lap. With many gentle and womanly offices, which none know better how to render than Mrs. Bird, the poor woman is in time rendered more calm. A temporary bed is provided for her on a settle, and in a short time she falls into a heavy slumber, with the child, who seems no less weary, soundly sleeping on her arm; for the mother resists with nervous anxiety the kindest attempts to take him from her, and even in sleep her arm encircles him with an unrelaxing clasp.]

MR. BIRD.

[aside, to his wife.]

I wonder who and what she is?

MRS. BIRD.

When she wakes up and feels a little rested, we will see.

MR. BIRD.

[after musing in silence.]
   I say, wife!

MRS. BIRD.

   Well, dear?

MR. BIRD.

   She could n't wear one of your gowns, could she,
by any letting down, or such matter? She seems
to be rather larger than you are.

MRS. BIRD.

[with a smile.]
   We 'll see.

MR. BIRD.

[after a pause.]
   I say, wife!

MRS. BIRD.

   Well! What now?

MR. BIRD.

   Why, there 's that old bombazine cloak that you
keep on purpose to put over me when I take my
afternoon's nap; you might as well give her that;
she needs clothes.

MRS. BIRD.

   Very well, dear! I 'll see what I can do!

   Exeunt Mr. and Mrs. Bird. Curtain falls.

SCENE III. *The same.*

[The woman sits upon the settle, looking steadily into the fire with a calm, heart-broken expression, very different from her former agitated wildness.]

Curtain rises on Eliza, the boy, Dinah and Cudjoe.
Enter Mr. and Mrs. Bird.

MRS. BIRD.

[in gentle tones.]

Did you want me ? I hope you feel better now, poor woman !

[A long-drawn, shivering sigh is the only answer ; but Eliza lifts her dark eyes and fixes them on Mrs. Bird with such a forlorn and imploring expression, that the tears come into the little woman's eyes.]

You need n't be afraid of anything ; we are friends here, poor woman ! Tell me where you came from, and what you want.

ELIZA.

I came from Kentucky.

MR. BIRD.

When ?

ELIZA.

To-night.

MR. BIRD.

How did you come ?

ELIZA.

I crossed on the ice.

MR. and MRS. BIRD, DINAH, and CUDJOE [together.]

Crossed on the ice !

ELIZA.

[slowly.]

Yes, I did. God helping me, I crossed on the ice ; for they were behind me — right behind — and there was no other way !

CUDJOE.

Law, missis, the ice is all in broken-up blocks, a-swinging and a-tetering up and down in the water !

ELIZA.

[wildly.]

I know it was ; I know it ! but I did it ! I would n't have thought I could. I did n't think I should get over ; but I did n't care ! I could but die if I did n't. The Lord helped me ; nobody knows how much the Lord can help 'em till they try.

MR. BIRD.

Were you a slave ?

ELIZA.

Yes, sir ; I belonged to a man in Kentucky.

MR. BIRD.

Was he unkind to you?

ELIZA.

No, sir; he was a good master.

MR. BIRD.

And was your mistress unkind to you?

ELIZA.

No, sir; no! My mistress was always good to me.

MR. BIRD.

What could induce you to leave a good home, then, and run away, and go through such dangers?

[The woman looks at Mrs. Bird with a keen, scrutinizing glance, and it does not escape her that she is dressed in deep mourning.]

ELIZA.

[suddenly.]

Ma'am, have you ever lost a child?

[The question is unexpected, and it is a thrust on a new wound; for it is only a month since a darling child of the family was laid in the grave. Mr. Bird turns round and walks to the window, and Mrs. Bird bursts into tears, but recovers her voice.]

MRS. BIRD.

Why do you ask that? I have lost a little one.

ELIZA.

Then you will feel for me. I have lost two, one
after another ; left them buried there when I came
away : and I had only this one left. I never slept
a night without him ; he was all I had. He was my
comfort and pride. day and night; and, ma'am,
they were going to take him away from me, — to
sell him ; sell him down south, ma'am, to go all
alone, — a baby that had never been away from his
mother in his life! I could n't stand it, ma'am. I
knew I never should be good for anything if they
did : and when I knew the papers were signed,
and he was sold, I took him and came off in the
night : and they chased me, — the man that bought
him and some of Mas'rs folks ; and they were coming down right behind me, and I heard 'em. I
jumped right on to the ice ; and how I got across
I don't know : but, first I knew a man was helping
me up the bank.

[The woman does not sob nor weep ; but every one around
her is showing signs of hearty sympathy. The two little
boys, after a desperate rummaging in their pockets in search
of those pocket-handkerchiefs which mothers know are never
to be found there, throw themselves into the skirts of their
mother's gown, where they sob and wipe their eyes to their
hearts' content. Mrs. Bird had her face fairly hidden in her
pocket-handkerchief, and old Dinah, letting the tears stream
down her black, honest face.]

DINAH.

Lord, have mercy on us!

[Old Cudjoe, rubbing his eyes very hard with his cuffs,

and making a most uncommon variety of wry faces, occasionally responds in the same key with great fervor.]

CUDJOE.

Lord, have mercy on us!

[Our senator is a statesman, and of course cannot be expected to cry like other mortals; and so he turns his back to the company and seems particularly busy in clearing his throat and wiping his spectacle glasses, occasionally blowing his nose in a manner that is calculated to excite suspicion.]

MR. BIRD.

[turning suddenly round upon the woman.]

How came you to tell me you had a kind master?

ELIZA.

Because he *was* a kind master. I 'll say that of him, anyway; and my mistress was kind; but they could n't help themselves. They were owing money, and there was some way, I can't tell how, that a man had a hold on them, and they were obliged to give him his will. I listened and heard him telling mistress that, and she begging and pleading for me; and he told her he couldn't help himself and that the papers were all drawn. And then it was I took him and left my home and came away; I knew 't was no use of my trying to live if they did it, for 't 'pears like this child is all I have.

MR. BIRD.

Have you no husband?

ELIZA.

Yes, but he belongs to another man. His master is real hard to him, and won't let him come to see me, hardly ever; and he 's grown harder and harder upon us, and he threatens to sell him down south. It' s like I 'll never see *him* again.

MRS. BIRD.

And where do you mean to go, my poor woman?

ELIZA.

[looking up with a simple, confiding air to Mrs. Bird's face.]

To Canada, if I only knew where that was. Is it very far off, is Canada?

MRS. BIRD.

[involuntarily.]

Poor thing!

ELIZA.

[earnestly.]

Is 't a very great way off, think?

MRS. BIRD.

Much farther than you think, poor child! But we will try to think what can be done for you. Here, Dinah, make her up a bed in your own room, close by the kitchen, and I 'll think what to do for her in the morning. Meanwhile, never fear, poor woman. Put your trust in God. He will protect you.

Curtain falls.

SCENE IV. *The parlor.*

Curtain rises.

[Mrs. Bird and her husband have reëntered the parlor. She sits in her little rocking-chair, swaying thoughtfully to and fro. Mr. Bird strides up and down the room grumbling to himself.]

MR. BIRD.

Pish ! pshaw ! confounded awkward business !

[At length striding up to his wife.]

I say, wife, she 'll have to get away from here this very night. That fellow will be down on the scent bright and early to-morrow morning. If 't was only the woman, she could lie quiet till it was over ; but that little chap can't be kept still by a troop of horse and foot, I 'll warrant me. He 'll bring it all out, popping his head out of some window or door. A pretty kettle of fish it would be for me, too, to be caught with them both here, just now. No ; they 'll have to be got off to-night.

MRS. BIRD.

To-night ! How is it possible ? Where to ?

MR. BIRD.

Well, I know pretty well where to.

[The senator begins to put on his boots with a reflective
air ; and stopping when his leg is half in, embraces his
knee with both hands, and seems to go off in deep meditation ; at last beginning to tug at his bootstraps again.
After one boot is fairly on, the senator sits with the other
in his hand, profoundly studying the figure of the carpet.]

It's a confounded, awkward, ugly business ; and
that's a fact!   It will have to be done, though, for
aught I see,— hang it all !

[and he draws the other boot anxiously on and looks out of
the window.]

You see, there's my old client, Van Trompe, has
come over from Kentucky, and set all his slaves
free ; and he has bought a place seven miles up the
creek, here, back in the woods, where nobody goes,
unless they go on purpose ; and it's a place that
isn't found in a hurry.   There she'd be safe
enough ; but the plague of the thing is, nobody
could drive a carriage there to-night but *me.*

MRS. BIRD.

Why not?   Cudjoe is an excellent driver.

MR. BIRD.

Ay, ay, but here it is.   The creek has to be
crossed twice, and the second crossing is quite dan-
gerous, unless one knows it as I do.   I have crossed

it a hundred times on horseback, and know exactly
the turns to take. And so, you see, there's no help
for it. Cudjoe must put in the horses, as quietly
as may be, about twelve o'clock, and I'll take her
over; and then, to give color to the matter, he must
carry me on to the next tavern, to take the stage
for Columbus, that comes by about three or four,
and so it will look as if I had the carriage only for
that. I shall get into business bright and early in
the morning. But I'm thinking I shall feel rather
cheap there, after all that's been said and done;
but hang it, I can't help it!

MRS. BIRD.

[laying her little white hand on his.]

Your heart is better than your head in this case,
John. Could I ever have loved you, had I not
known you better than you know yourself?

[Mr. Bird walks off soberly to see about the carriage.
At the door, however, he stops a moment, and then coming
back, speaks with some hesitation.]

MR. BIRD.

Mary, I don't know how you'd feel about it, but
there's that drawer full of things — of — of — poor
little Henry's.

[So saying, he turns quickly on his heel and shuts the door
after him.]

*Exit Mrs. Bird, followed by the two boys. In a minute or two, she returns
carrying a small bundle of clothing.*

TOM.

[gently touching her arm.]

Mamma, are you going to give away *those* things?

MRS. BIRD.

[softly and earnestly.]

My dear boys, if our dear loving little Henry looks down from heaven, he would be glad to have us do this. I could not find it in my heart to give them away to any common person — to anybody that was happy ; but I give them to a mother more heart-broken and sorrowful than I am, and I hope God will send His blessings with them.

[Mrs. Bird has also brought out a plain, serviceable dress or two, and she sits down busily to her work-table, and with needle, scissors, and thimble at hand, quietly commences the "letting-down" process, which her husband had recommended, and continues busily at it, till the old clock strikes twelve, and she hears the low rattling of wheels at the door.]

MR. BIRD.

[coming in with his overcoat in his hand.]

Mary, you must wake her up now ; we must be off.

Curtain falls.

SCENE V. *Another kitchen.*

[John van Trompe is a great, tall, bristling Orson of a fellow, full six feet and some inches in his stockings, and arrayed in a red flannel hunting-shirt. A very heavy *mat* of sandy hair, in a decidedly tousled condition, and a beard of some days' growth, give the worthy man an appearance, to say the least, not particularly prepossessing. He stands for a few minutes holding the candle aloft, and blinking on our travellers with a dismal and mystified expression that is truly ludicrous. It costs some effort of our senator to induce him to comprehend the case fully.]

Curtain rises on Mr. Bird and Van Trompe.

MR. BIRD.

Are you the man that will shelter a poor woman and child from slave-catchers?

VAN TROMPE.

[with considerable emphasis.] ·

I rather think I am.

MR. BIRD.

I thought so.

VAN TROMPE.

[stretching his tall muscular form upward.]

If there's anybody comes, why, here I am ready for him; and I've got seven sons, each six foot high, and they'll be ready for 'em. Give our respects to 'em, tell 'em it's no matter how soon they call, — make no kinder difference to us.

[running his fingers through the shock of hair that thatches his head, and bursting out into a great laugh.]

Exit Mr. Bird, returning with Eliza and her child.

[Weary, jaded, and spiritless, Eliza drags herself in, with her child lying in a heavy sleep on her arm. The rough man holds a candle to her face and utters a kind of compassionate grunt.]

VAN TROMPE to ELIZA.

Now, I say, gal, you need n't be a bit afeard, let
who will come here; I 'm up to all that sort o' thing,
[pointing to two or three goodly rifles on the wall.]
and most people that know me know that 't would
n't be healthy to try to get anybody out o' my house
when I 'm agin it. So *now* you jist go to sleep
now, as quiet as if yer mother was a-rockin' you.
[taking down a candle and lighting it, he gives it to
Eliza.]

This way, my gal.

Exit Van Trompe, followed by Eliza. Reënter Van Trompe.

VAN TROMPE.

Poor crittur, hunted down now like a deer;
hunted down jest for havin' natural feelins and
doin' what no kind o' mother could help a-doin'!
I tell ye what, these yer things make me come the
nighest to swearin', now, o' most anything.
[wiping his eyes with the back of a great freckled, yellow
hand.]

I tell yer what, stranger, it was years and years before I 'd jine the church, 'cause the ministers round
in our parts used to preach that the Bible went in
for these 'ere cuttings-up, and I could n't be up to
'em with their Greek and Hebrew, and so I took
agin 'em, Bible and all. I never jined the church
till I found a minister that was up to 'em all in
Greek and all that, and he said right the contrary;

and then I took right hold, and jined the church ; I did, now, fact.

[all this time uncorking some very frisky bottled cider, which at this juncture he presents.]

You had better jest put up here, now, till daylight, and I'll call up the old woman, and have a bed got ready for you in no time.

MR. BIRD.

Thank you, my good friend ; I must be along, to take the night stage for Columbus.

[At this point, the senator puts into Van Trompe's hand a ten-dollar bill.]

It's for her.

VAN TROMPE.

Ay, ay.

[They shake hands and part.]

Curtain falls.

THE WAY *SHE* "WAS RAISED."

CHARACTERS.

Miss Asphyxia Smith.
Miss Mehitable Rossiter.
Mrs. Badger.
Miss Lois Badger, daughter to Mrs. Badger.
Mrs. Smith, sister-in-law to Miss Asphyxia.
Tina Percival, a little girl.

COSTUMES.

Plainly made stuff skirts and bodices, with aprons and close-fitting caps for Mrs. Smith and Mrs. Badger. Miss Mehitable and Miss Asphyxia must wear large old-fashioned bonnets and shawls. Miss Lois, stuff skirt, cotton short gown and apron. Tina, a plain, short dress and white pinafore and bonnet.

ANALYSIS OF SCENES: PROPERTIES.

Scene I. A kitchen with exit. Miss Asphyxia takes Tina to "raise."

Properties. Kitchen furniture. A doughnut.

Scene II. Room with exit. Miss Asphyxia gives Tina up to Miss Mehitable.

Properties. Chairs, table, etc. Knitting-work and needles. A small bundle of homespun clothing.

SCENE I.   *A kitchen.*

Curtain rises on Miss Asphyxia, Mrs. Smith, and Tina.

MISS ASPHYXIA.

There won't be no great profit in this 'ere, these ten year.

[The object denominated "this 'ere" is a golden-haired child of seven years. Miss Asphyxia Smith is at this moment turning the child round, and examining her through a pair of large horn spectacles, with a view to "taking her to raise" as she phrases it. . . . Miss Asphyxia is tall and spare. Nature had made her, as she often remarked of herself, entirely for use. She had allowed for her muscles no cushioned repose of fat, no redundant smoothness of outline. There is nothing to her but good, strong, solid bone, and tough, wiry, well-strung muscle. She is past fifty, and her hair is already well streaked with gray. . . . She brushes up a handful of Tina's clustering curls in her large, bony hand, saying, with a sniff :]

These 'll have to come right off to begin with ; gracious me, what a tangle !

TINA.

Mother always brushed them out every day.

MISS ASPHYXIA.

And who do you suppose is going to spend an hour every day brushing your hair, Miss Pert ? That ain't what I take ye for, I tell you.   You 've got to learn to work for your living ; and you ought to be thankful if I 'm willing to show you how.

[The little girl does not appear particularly thankful.   She bends her soft, pencilled eyebrows in a dark frown, and her great hazel eyes have gathered in them a cloud of sullen gloom. Miss Asphyxia does not mind her frowning, — perhaps does not notice it. She had it settled in her mind, as a first principle, that children never liked anything that was good for them, and that, of course, if she took a child, it would have to be made to come to her by forcible proceedings promptly instituted. So she sets her little subject before her by seizing her by her two shoulders, and squaring her round, and looking in her face, and opens direct conversation with her in the following succinct manner.]

What's your name?

[Then follows a resolved and gloomy silence, as the large bright eyes survey, with a sort of defiant glance, the inquisitor.]

Don't you hear?
[giving her a shake.]

MRS. SMITH.

[taking the child's hand.]

Don't be so ha'sh with her! Say, my little dear, tell Miss Asphyxia your name!

TINA.

[turning towards the old woman, disdaining to answer the other party in the conversation.]

Eglantine Percival.

MISS ASPHYXIA.

Wh-a-t! If there ain't the beaten'est name ever I heard. Well, I tell you, *I* ain't got time to fix *my* mouth to say all that 'ere every time I want ye, now I tell ye!

TINA.

Mother and Harry called me Tina.

MISS ASPHYXIA.

Teny! Well, I should think so! That showed she'd got a grain o' sense left, anyhow. She's tol'able strong and well-limbed for her age,

[feeling of the child's arms and limbs ;]

her flesh is solid. I think she'll make a strong woman, only put her to work early and keep her at it. I could rub out clothes at the wash-tub afore I was at her age.

MRS. SMITH.

Oh, she can do considerable many little chores.

MISS ASPHYXIA.

Yes, there can a good deal be got out of a child if you keep at 'em, hold 'em in tight, and never let 'em have their head a minute ; push right hard on behind 'em, and you get considerable. That's the way *I* was raised.

TINA.

But I want to play.

[bursting out in a sobbing storm of mingled fear and grief.]

MISS ASPHYXIA.

Want to play, do you? Well, you must get over that. Don't you know that that's as bad as stealing? You have n't got any money, and if you eat folks's bread and butter, you 've got to work to pay for it; and if folks buy your clothes, you 've got to work to pay for them.

TINA.

But I 've got some clothes of my own.

MISS ASPHYXIA.

Well, so you have; but there ain't no sort of wear in 'em.

[turning to Mrs. Smith.]

Them two dresses o' hern might answer for Sundays and sich, but I 'll have to make her up a regular linsey working-dress this fall, and check aprons; and she must set right about knitting every minute she is n't doing anything else. Did you ever learn how to knit?

TINA.

No.

MISS ASPHYXIA.

Or to sew?

TINA.

Yes; mother taught me to sew.

MISS ASPHYXIA.

No! Yes! Hain't you learned manners? Do you say yes and no to people?

[The child stands a moment, swelling with suppressed feeling, and at last opens her great eyes full on Miss Asphyxia.]

TINA.

I don't like you. You ain't pretty, and I won't go with you.

MRS. SMITH.

Oh now! little girls must n't talk so ; that 's naughty.

MISS ASPHYXIA.

[with a short, grim laugh.]

Don't like me? — ain't I pretty? Maybe I ain't; but I know what I 'm about, and you 'd as good 's know it first as last. I 'm going to take ye right out with me in the waggin, and you 'd best not have none of your cuttins up. I keep a stick at home for naughty girls. Why, where do you suppose you 're going to get your livin' if I don't take you ?

TINA.

[sobbing.]

I want to live with Harry. Where is Harry ?

MISS ASPHYXIA.

Harry 's to work, — and there 's where he 's got to be. He 's got to work with the men in the fields, and you 've got to come home and work with me.

TINA.

[in a piteous tone.]

I want to stay with Harry.   Harry takes care
of me.

Exit Mrs. Smith, to return immediately with a doughnut.

MRS. SMITH.

There now, eat that, and mebbe, if you 're good,
Miss Asphyxia will bring you down here sometime.

MISS ASPHYXIA.

O laws, Polly, you allers was a fool! It 's all
for the child's good, and what's the use of fussin'
on her up?   She 'll come to it when she knows
she 's got to.   'T ain't no more than I was put to
at her age, only the child 's been fooled with and
babied.

[The little one refuses the doughnut, and seems to gather
herself up in silent gloom.]

Come now, don't stand sulking ; let me put your
bonnet on.

[in a brisk metallic voice.]

I can't be losing the best part of my day with
this nonsense !

MRS. SMITH.

Be a good girl, now ; be a good girl, and do just
as she tells you to.

MISS ASPHYXIA.

I 'll see to that !

Exit Miss Asphyzia, holding Tina by the hand.

Curtain falls.

SCENE II.   *Room in Mrs. Badger's house.*

[Miss Mehitable is making a quiet call at my grandmother's, and the party, consisting of grandmother (Mrs. Badger),
Aunt Lois, and herself, are peacefully rattling their knit-
ting-needles, while Tina is playing by the riverside, when the
child's senses are suddenly paralyzed by the sight of Miss
Asphyxia driving with a strong arm over the bridge.]

Curtain rises on Mrs. Badger, Aunt Lois, and Miss Mehitable.

[Tina runs in at the back door, perfectly pale with fright,
and seizes hold imploringly of Miss Mehitable's gown.]

Enter Tina.

TINA.

Oh, she 's coming ! she 's coming after me.   Don't
let her get me !

MRS. BADGER.

What 's the matter now ?   What ails the child ?

[Miss Mehitable lifts her in her lap, and the child clings
to her, reiterating:]

TINA.

Don't let her have me ! She 's dreadful ! Don't!

AUNT LOIS.

[who has tripped to the window.]

As true as you live, mother, there's Miss Asphyxia Smith hitching her horse at our picket fence!

MRS. BADGER.

[squaring her shoulders and setting herself in fine martial order.]

She is? Well, let her come in ; she's welcome, I'm sure. I'd like to talk to that woman! It's a free country, and everybody's got to speak their minds.

[and my grandmother rattles her needles with great energy.]

Enter Miss Asphyxia.

MISS ASPHYXIA.

Good day, Mis' Badger! How d'ye do, Miss Rossiter? Good day, Miss Lois!

[She is arrayed in her best Sunday clothes, and makes the neighborly salutations with an air of grim composure.]

MISS MEHITABLE and AUNT LOIS.

Good day, Miss Smith!

MRS. BADGER.

Glad to see you, Miss Asphyxia. Pray sit down!

Miss Asphyxia seats herself.

[There is silence and a sense of something brooding in the air, as there often is before the outburst of a storm. Finally, Miss Asphyxia opens the trenches.]

MISS ASPHYXIA.

I come over, Mis' Badger, to see about a gal o' mine that has run away.

[Here her eye rests severely on Tina.]

MRS. BADGER.

[briskly.]

Run away! and good reason she should run away; all I wonder at is that you have the face to come to a Christian family after her, — that's all. Well, she is provided for, and you've no call to be inquiring anything about *her*. So I advise you to go home and attend to your own affairs, and leave children to folks that know how to manage them better than you do.

MISS ASPHYXIA.

[in towering wrath.]

I expected this, Mis' Badger, but I'd have you to know that I ain't a person that's going to take sa'ace from no one. No deacon nor deacon's wife nor perfessor of religion 's agoin' to turn up their noses at me! I can hold up my head with any on 'em, and I think your religion might teach you better than takin' up stories agin your neighbors as a little, lyin', artful hussy 'll tell.

[Here there is a severe glance at Miss Tina, who quails before it and clings to Miss Mehitable's gown.]

Yes indeed, you may hide your head, but you can't git away from the truth; not when I 'm round

to bring you out. Yes, Mis' Badger, I defy her to
say I hain't done well by her, if she says the truth,
for I say it now, this blessed minute, and would say
it on my dyin'-bed, and you can ask Sol ef that 'ere
child hain't had everything pervided for her that a
child could want, — a good clean bed and plenty o'
bedclothes, and good whole clothes to wear, and lots
o' good victuals every day; an' me a-teachin' and a-
trainin' on her, enough to wear the very life out o'
me, — for I always hated young uns, and this 'ere 's
a perfect little limb as I ever did see. Why what
did she think I was agoin' to do for her? I did n't
make a lady on her; to be sure I did n't. I was
a-fetchin' her up to work for her livin' as I was
fetched up. I had n't nothin' more 'n she; an'
just look at me now; there ain't many folks can
turn off as much work in a day as I can, though I
say it that should n't. And I 've got as pretty a
piece of property, and as well seen to, as most any
round; and all I 've got — house and lands — is
my own arnins, honest, — so there!

[Here Miss Asphyxia elevates her nose and sniffs over
my grandmother's cap-border in a very contemptuous manner, and the cap-border bristles defiantly but undismayed
back again.]

Come now, Mis' Badger, have it out; I ain't
afraid of you! I 'd just like to have you tell me
what I could ha' done more nor better for this
child.

MRS. BADGER.

Done !

[with a pop like a roasted chestnut bursting out of the fire.]

Why you've done what you'd no business to. You'd no business to take a child at all; you haven't got a grain of motherliness in you. Why, look at natur', that might teach you that more than meat and drink and clothes is wanted for a child. Hens brood their chickens, and keep 'em warm under their wings, and cows lick their calves and cosset 'em, and it's a mean shame that folks will take 'em away from them. 'T ain't just feedin' and clothin' that's all; it's *broodin'* that young creeturs wants; and you hain't got a bit of broodin' in you; your heart's as hard as the nether millstone. Sovereign grace may soften it some day, but nothin' else can. You're a poor, old, hard, worldly woman, Miss Asphyxia Smith; that's what *you* are! If Divine grace could have broken in upon you, and given you a heart to love the child, you might have brought her up, 'cause you are a smart woman, and an honest one; that nobody denies.

MISS MEHITABLE.

[in conciliatory tones.]

My good Miss Smith, by your own account you must have had a great deal of trouble with this child. Now I propose for the future to relieve you of it altogether. I do not think you would ever succeed in making as efficient a person as yourself of her.   I don't doubt you conscientiously intended to do your duty by her, and I beg you to believe that you need have no further trouble with her.

MISS ASPHYXIA.

Goodness gracious knows, the child ain't much to fight over, — she was nothin' but a plague ; and I 'd rather have done all she did any day, than to 'a' had her round under my feet.   I hate young uns, anyway.

MISS MEHITABLE.

Then why, my good woman, do you object to parting with her ?

MISS ASPHYXIA.

Who said I did object?   I don't care nothin' about parting with her ; all is, when I begin a thing I like to go through with it.

MISS MEHITABLE.

But if it is n't worth while going through with, it 's as well to leave it, is it not ?

MISS ASPHYXIA.

And I 'd got her clothes made, — not that they 're worth so very much, but then they 're worth just what they *are* worth, anyway.

Exit Tina to reënter immediately.

[Here Tina made a sudden impulsive dart from Miss Mehitable's lap and ran out of the back door, and over to her new home, and up into the closet of the chamber, where was hanging the new suit of homespun in which Miss Asphyxia had arrayed her. She took it down and rolled the articles all together in a tight bundle, which she secured with a string, and, before the party in the kitchen had ceased wondering at her flight, suddenly reappeared, with flushed cheeks and dilated eyes, and tossed the bundle into Miss Asphyxia's lap.]

TINA.

There's every bit you ever gave me; I don't want to keep a single thing!

MISS MEHITABLE.

[reprovingly.]
My dear, is that a proper way to speak?

MISS ASPHYXIA.

[rising.]
Well, it's no use talking. If folks think they're able to bring up a beggar child like a lady, it's their lookout and not mine. I wasn't aware
[she added with severe irony.]
that Parson Rossiter left so much of an estate that you could afford to bring up other folks's children in silks and satins.

MISS MEHITABLE.

[good-naturedly.]
Our estate isn't much, but we shall make the best of it.

MISS ASPHYXIA.

Well now, you just mark my words, Miss Rossiter, that 'ere child will never grow up a smart
woman with *your* bringin' up ; she'll jest run right
over *you* and you'll let her have her head in everything. I see jest how 't'll be ; I don't want nobody
to tell me.

MISS MEHITABLE.

I dare say you are quite right, Miss Smith; I
have n't the slightest opinion of my own powers in
that line; but she may be happy with me, for all
that.

MISS ASPHYXIA.

[with an odd intonation, as if repeating a sound of something imperfectly comprehended.]

Happy? Oh, well, if folks is goin' to begin to
talk about *that*, I hain't got time ; it don't seem to
me, that *that's* what this 'ere world's for.

MISS MEHITABLE.

What is it for, then ?

MISS ASPHYXIA.

Meant for? Why, for hard work, I s'pose;
that's all I ever found it for. Talk about cod-
dling ! it's little we get o' that in this world, dear
knows. You must take things right off when
they're goin'. Ef you don't, so much the worse

for you ; they won't wait for you. Lose an hour in
the morning, and you may chase it till ye drop
down, you 'll never catch it! That 's the way
things goes, and I should like to know who 's agoing
to stop to quiddle with young uns? 'T ain't me,
that 's certain. So as there 's no more to be made
by this 'ere talk, I may as well be goin'. You 're
welcome to the young un, ef you say so. I jest
wanted you to know that what I 'd begun I 'd 'a'
gone through with, ef you had n't stepped in ; and
I did n't want no reflections on my good name,
neither, for I had *my* ideas of what 's right and can
have 'em yet, I s'pose, if Mis' Badger does think
I 've got a heart of stone!

MISS MEHITABLE.

Well, well, Miss Smith, I respect your motives,
and would be happy to see you any time you will
call, and I 'm in hopes to teach this little girl to
treat you properly.

[taking the child's hand.]

MISS ASPHYXIA.

[with a short, hard laugh.]

Likely story. She 'll get ahead o' you, you 'll
see that ; but I don't hold malice, so good morning.

[and Miss Asphyxia suddenly and promptly departs and is
soon seen driving away at a violent pace.]

Exit Miss Asphyxia.

MISS MEHITABLE.

Upon my word, that woman is n't so bad now !

TINA.

Oh, I 'm so glad you did n't let her have me !

Curtain falls.

DINAH'S KITCHEN.

CHARACTERS.

AUGUSTINE ST. CLARE, the master of the house.
MISS OPHELIA ST. CLARE (cousin to St. Clare) — acting as housekeeper.
DINAH, a negress, and the cook.
SAM, JAKE (negro boys), and other slaves.

COSTUMES.

ST. CLARE must wear a suit of clothes suitable for morning wear in a warm climate.

MISS OPHELIA. A plain, full-skirted dress, with large serviceable apron. Hair parted and arranged simply.

DINAH. A bright, printed cotton dress, with apron; both dress and apron soiled and untidy.

SAM, JAKE, and the other slaves, carelessly dressed in cool materials.

ANALYSIS OF SCENES: PROPERTIES.

SCENE I. Kitchen in ST. CLARE's house with exit (and fireplace if possible). MISS OPHELIA puts the kitchen in order.

PROPERTIES. Chairs, tables, chest of drawers. Potatoes, fowls, and peas, if possible. Pudding-stick. Table-cloth badly stained, — nutmeg-grater; saucer of pomade; — table-napkins; onions in piece of flannel, — papers of sweet herbs. (The rest of the articles described as being found in drawer in Scene I. are not necessary but will be appropriate.) Sugar-bowl, plates, basins,

towels, etc. ; pipe of tobacco.   In this scene, everything must be
disordered and out of place.

SCENE II. Parlor in ST. CLARE's house.   Conversation between
ST. CLARE and MISS OPHELIA.

PROPERTIES. Carpet, curtains, pictures, ornaments, and furniture suitable for parlor, and bell.

SCENE I.   *The kitchen.*

[It is now the season of incipient preparation for dinner.
Dinah, who requires large intervals of reflection and repose,
and is studious of ease in all her arrangements, is seated
on the kitchen-floor, smoking a short, stumpy pipe, to which
she is much addicted.   Seated round her are various members of that rising race with which a Southern household
abounds, engaged in shelling peas, peeling potatoes, picking
pin-feathers out of fowls, and other preparatory arrangements, — Dinah every once in a while interrupting her med-
itations to give a poke, or a rap on the head, to some of the
young operators, with the pudding-stick that lies by her side.

The kitchen is a large, brick - floored apartment, with a
great old - fashioned fireplace stretching along one side of
it.   When St. Clare had first returned from the North, im-
pressed with the system and order of his uncle's kitchen
arrangements, he had largely provided his own with an array
of cupboards, drawers, and various apparatus, under the san-
guine illusion that it would be of any possible assistance to
Dinah in her arrangements. . . . Her   kitchen   generally
looks as if it had been arranged by a hurricane blowing
through it, and she has about as many places for each cook-
ing utensil as there are days in the year.]

Curtain rises on Dinah and her Assistants.

Enter Miss Ophelia.

[When Miss Ophelia enters the kitchen, on her reformatory tour through the establishment, Dinah does not rise but smokes on in sublime tranquillity, regarding her movements obliquely out of the corner of her eye, but apparently intent only on the operations around her. Miss Ophelia commences opening a set of drawers.]

MISS OPHELIA.

What is this drawer for, Dinah?

DINAH.

It 's handy for most anything, missis.

[So it appears to be. From the variety it contains Miss Ophelia pulls out first a fine damask table - cloth stained with blood, having evidently been used to envelop some raw meat.]

MISS OPHELIA.

What 's this, Dinah? You don't wrap up meat in your mistress's best table-cloths?

DINAH.

O Lor, missis, no ; the towels was all a-missin', — so I jest did it. I laid out to wash that 'ar, — that 's why I put it thar.

MISS OPHELIA.

[to herself.]

Shiftless !

[Proceeding to tumble over the drawer, she finds a nutmeg-grater and two or three nutmegs, a small Methodist hymn-book, a couple of soiled Madras handkerchiefs, some yarn and knitting-work, a paper of tobacco and a pipe, a few crackers, one or two gilded china saucers with some pomade

in them, one or two thin old shoes, a piece of flannel carefully pinned up, inclosing some small white onions, several
damask table-napkins, some coarse crash towels, some twine
and darning-needles, and several broken papers from which
sundry sweet herbs are sifting into the drawer.]

Where do you keep your nutmegs, Dinah?
[with the air of one who prays for patience.]

DINAH.

Most anywhar, missis; there's some in that
cracked teacup, up there, and there's some over
in that ar cupboard.

MISS OPHELIA.

[holding them up.]
Here are some in the grater.

DINAH.

Laws, yes; I put 'em thar this morning. I likes
to keep my things handy. You, Jake! what are
you stopping for? You'll cotch it! Be still,
thar!
[with a dive of her stick at the criminal.]

MISS OPHELIA.

[holding up the saucer of pomade.]
What's this?

DINAH.

Laws, it's my har-grease. I put it thar to have
it handy.

MISS OPHELIA.

Do you use your mistress's best saucers for that?

DINAH.

Law, it was 'cause I was driv, and in sich a hurry; I was gwine to change it this very day.

MISS OPHELIA.

Here are two damask table-napkins.

DINAH.

Them table-napkins I put thar, to get 'em washed out some day.

MISS OPHELIA.

Don't you have some place here on purpose for things to be washed?

DINAH.

Well, Mas'r St. Clare got dat ar chest, he said, for dat; but I likes to mix up biscuit and hev my things on it some days, and then it ain't handy a-liftin' up the lid.

MISS OPHELIA.

Why don't you mix your biscuits on the pastry table there?

DINAH.

Laws, missis, it gets sot so full of dishes, and one thing and another, der ain't no room, noways —

But you should *wash* your dishes, and clear them away.

DINAH.

[in a high key, as her wrath begins to rise over her habitual respect of manner.]

Wash my dishes? What does ladies know 'bout work, I want to know? When 'd Mas'r ever get his dinner if I was to spend all my time a-washin' and a-puttin' up dishes? Miss Marie never telled me so, nohow.

MISS OPHELIA.

Well, here are these onions.   •

DINAH.

Laws, yes! thar *is* whar I put 'em, now. I could n't 'member. Them's particular onions I was a-savin' for dis yer very stew. I'd forgot they was in dat ar old flannel.

[Miss Ophelia lifts out the sifting papers of sweet herbs.]

I wish missis would n't touch dem ar. I likes to keep my things where I knows whar to go to 'em. [rather decidedly.]

MISS OPHELIA.

But you don't want these holes in the papers.

DINAH.

Them's handy for siftin' on 't out.

MISS OPHELIA.

But you see it spills all over the drawer.

DINAH.

Laws, yes ! if missis will go a-tumblin' things all up so, it will.   Missis has spilt lots dat ar way.

[coming uneasily to the drawers.]

If missis will only go upstars till my clarin'-up time comes, I have every thing right ; but I can't do nothin' when ladies is round a-henderin'.   You Sam, don't you touch dat ar sugar-bowl ! I 'll crack ye over if ye don't mind.

MISS OPHELIA.

I 'm going through the kitchen, and going to put everything in order, *once*, Dinah, and then I 'll expect you to *keep* it so.

DINAH.

Lor, now ! Miss Phelia ; dat ar ain't no way for ladies to do.   I never did see ladies doin' no sich ; my old missis nor Miss Marie never did, and I don't see no kinder need on 't.

[and Dinah stalks indignantly about, while Miss Ophelia piles and sorts dishes, empties dozens of scattering sugar-bowls into one receptacle, sorts napkins, table-cloths, and towels for washing ; washing, wiping, and arranging with her own hands, and with a speed and alacrity that perfectly amazes Dinah.]

DINAH.

[to some of her satellites, when at a safe hearing distance.]

Lor, now! if dat ar de way dem northern ladies do, dey ain't ladies nohow. I has things as straight as anybody, when my clarin'-up time comes, but I don't want ladies round a-henderin' and getting my things all where I can't find 'em.

Curtain falls.

SCENE II. *A parlor.*

[Miss Ophelia, in a few days, thoroughly reformed every department of the house to a systematic pattern ; but her labors in all departments that depended on the co-operation of servants were like those of Sisyphus or the Danaides. In despair, she one day appeals to St. Clare.]

Curtain rises on St. Clare and Miss Ophelia.

MISS OPHELIA.

There is no such thing as getting anything like system in this family !

ST. CLARE.

To be sure there is n't.

MISS OPHELIA.

Such shiftless management, such waste, such confusion, I never saw !

ST. CLARE.

I dare say you did n't.

MISS OPHELIA.

You would not take it so coolly if you were house-keeper.

ST. CLARE.

My dear cousin, you may as well understand once for all, that we masters are divided into two classes, oppressors and oppressed. We who are good-natured and hate severity make up our minds to a good deal of inconvenience. If we *will keep* a shambling, loose, untaught set in the community for our convenience, why, we must take the consequence. Some rare cases I have seen of persons who, by a peculiar tact, can produce order and system without severity; but I'm not one of them, — and so I made up my mind long ago to let things go just as they do. I will not have the poor creatures thrashed and cut to pieces, and they know it, — and, of course, they know the staff is in their own hands.

MISS OPHELIA.

But to have no time, no place, no order, — all going on in this shiftless way!

ST. CLARE.

My dear Vermont, you natives up by the North Pole set an extravagant value on time! What on earth is the use of time to a fellow who has twice as much of it as he knows what to do with? As to

order and system, where there is nothing to be done
but to lounge on the sofa and read, an hour sooner
or later in breakfast or dinner is n't of much account.   Now, there 's Dinah gets you a capital dinner, — soup, ragout, roast fowl, dessert, ice-creams,
and all, — and she creates it all out of chaos and
old night down there in that kitchen.   I think it
really sublime the way she manages.   But, Heaven
bless us ! if we are to go down there and view all
the smoking and squatting about, and hurry-scurry-
ation of the preparatory process, we should never
eat more !   My good cousin, absolve yourself from
that !   It 's more than a penance, and does no more
good.   You 'll only lose your own temper, and
utterly confound Dinah.   Let her go her own way.

MISS OPHELIA.

But, Augustine, you don't know how I found
things.

ST. CLARE.

Don't I ?   Don't I know that the rolling-pin is
under her bed, and the nutmeg-grater in her pocket
with her tobacco, — that there are sixty-five different sugar-bowls, one in every hole in the house, —
that she washes dishes with a dinner-napkin one
day, and with a fragment of an old petticoat the
next ?   But the upshot is, she gets up glorious
dinners, makes superb coffee ; and you must judge
her as warriors and statesmen are judged — by *her*
success.

MISS OPHELIA.

But the waste, — the expense!

ST. CLARE.

Oh, well! Lock everything you can, and keep the key. Give out by driblets, and never inquire for odds and ends, — it isn't best.

MISS OPHELIA.

That troubles me, Augustine. I can't help feeling as if these servants were not *strictly honest*. Are you sure they can be relied on?

[St. Clare laughs immoderately at the grave and anxious face with which Miss Ophelia propounds the question.]

ST. CLARE.

Oh, cousin, that's too good, — *honest!* — as if that's a thing to be expected! Honest! — why, of course they aren't. Why should they be? What upon earth is to make them so?

MISS OPHELIA.

Why don't you instruct?

ST. CLARE.

Instruct! Oh, fiddlesticks! What instructing do you think I should do? I look like it! As to Marie, she has spirit enough, to be sure, to kill off a whole plantation, if I'd let her manage; but she wouldn't get the cheatery out of them.

MISS OPHELIA.

Are there no honest ones?

ST. CLARE.

Well, now and then one, whom Nature makes so impracticably simple, truthful, and faithful, that the worst possible influence can't destroy it. But for my part, I don't see how they *can* be honest. Such a fellow, as Tom here is, is a moral miracle.

MISS OPHELIA.

And what becomes of their souls?

ST. CLARE.

That is n't my affair as I know of; I am only dealing in facts of the present life.

MISS OPHELIA.

This is perfectly horrible! You ought to be ashamed of yourselves.

ST. CLARE.

I don't know as I am. We are in pretty good company for all that, as people in the broad road generally are. Look at the high and low, all the world over, and it 's the same story — the lower class used up body, soul, and spirit, for the good of the upper. (*Bell rings.*) But there 's the bell, so, cousin, come out to dinner.

[*Exeunt both.*

Curtain falls.

WHO WOULD MARRY A MINISTER?

CHARACTERS.

MARY SCUDDER, who is engaged to Dr. Hopkins, the minister of Newport.

CERINTHY ANN TWITCHEL.

MRS. TWITCHEL, mother to Cerinthy.

MRS. JONES.

Other ladies and girls.

COSTUMES.

Skirts and "short-gowns" and aprons for all. Caps for the elder ladies. In Scene II. Cerinthy must wear an old-fashioned *straw bonnet*.

ANALYSIS OF SCENES: PROPERTIES.

SCENE I. An old-fashioned parlor with exit. A "quilting-bee" for Mary Scudder's wedding-quilt.

PROPERTIES. Mats, simple furniture, and ornaments. A quilt on a frame, needles, scissors, reels of thread, etc.

SCENE II. Same as in Scene I. Cerinthy asks Mary's advice about marrying a minister.

PROPERTIES. Same as in Scene I., omitting the quilt and frame. Also, a piece of sewing, and several damask table-napkins.

SCENE I. *Parlor in Mrs. Scudder's house.*

[By two o'clock a goodly company begins to assemble. The quilt-pattern is gloriously drawn in oak-leaves, done in indigo ; and soon all the company, young and old, are passing busy fingers over it, and conversation goes on briskly.]

Curtain rises.

CERINTHY ANN.

I never can see into it, how any girl can marry a minister !

MRS. TWITCHEL.

Oh, Cerinthy Ann ! how can you go on so ?

CERINTHY ANN.

It 's a fact ! Now other men let you have some peace, — but a minister is always round under your feet.

MRS. JONES.

So you think, the less you see of a husband the better ?

CERINTHY ANN.

[giving a decided snip to her thread with her scissors.]

Just my views. I like the Nantucketers, that go off on four-years' voyages and leave their wives a clear field. If ever I get married, I 'm going to have one of those fellows.

MRS. TWITCHEL.

You 'd better take care, Cerinthy Ann ; they say that " those who sing before breakfast will cry before supper." Girls talk about getting married, [relapsing into a gentle didactic melancholy.] without realizing its awful responsibilities.

CERINTHY ANN.

Oh, as to that, I 've been practising on my pudding now these six years, and I should n't be afraid to throw one up chimney with any girl.

[*All laugh.*

[This speech was founded on a tradition, current in those times, that no young lady was fit to be married till she could construct a boiled Indian pudding of such consistency that it could be thrown up chimney and come down on the ground, outside, without breaking ; and the consequence of Cerinthy Ann's sally was a general laugh.]

AN ELDERLY LADY.

[sententiously.]

Girls a'n't what they used to be in my day. I remember my mother told me when she was thirteen, she could knit a long cotton stocking in a day.

CERINTHY ANN.

[appealing to the younger members at the frame.]

I have n't much faith in these stories of old times, — have you, girls?

MRS. TWITCHEL.

At any rate, our minister's wife will be a pattern ; I don't know anybody that goes beyond her either in spinning or in fine stitching !

Curtain falls.

SCENE II. *The same.*

Curtain rises on Mary Scudder sewing.

[Suddenly the trip of a very brisk foot is heard in the kitchen, and Cerinthy Ann Twitchel makes her appearance at the door.]

MARY.

Why, Cerinthy, how glad I am to see you!

CERINTHY.

Well, I have been meaning to come down all this week, but there's so much to do in haying time, but to-day I told mother I *must* come. I brought these down,

[unfolding a dozen snowy napkins.]

that I spun myself, and was thinking of you almost all the while I spun them, so I suppose they are n't quite so wicked as they might be.

MARY.

Thank you, Cerinthy.   They are beautiful.

CERINTHY.

I don't see how you can keep so calm, when things are coming so near!

Mary smiles quietly.

I don't see, for my part, how a young girl *could* marry a minister, anyhow; but then I think *you* are just cut out for it.   But what *would* anybody say, if *I* should do such a thing?

MARY.

[innocently.]

I don't know.

CERINTHY.

Well, I suppose everybody would hold up their hands; and yet, if I *do* say it myself, there are not many girls who could make a better minister's wife than I could, if I had a mind to try.

[coloring.]

MARY.

[warmly.]

That I am sure of.

CERINTHY.

[giving an impatient toss.]

I guess you are the only one that ever thought so. There's father and mother all the while mourning over me; and yet I don't see but what I do pretty much all that is done in the house, and they say I am a great comfort in a temporal point of view. But oh, the groanings and the sighings that there are over me! I don't think it is pleasant to know that your best friends are thinking such awful things about you, when you are working your fingers off to help them. It is kind o' discouraging, but I don't know what to do about it.

[and for a few moments Cerinthy sits silent, while her cheeks grow redder with something that she is going to say next.]

Now, Mary, there is *that creature.* Well, you know, he won't take " No " for an answer. What shall I do?

MARY.

[rather archly.]

Suppose then you try " Yes."

CERINTHY.

Oh, pshaw ! Mary Scudder, you know better than that now. I look like it, don't I ?

MARY.

[looking at Cerinthy deliberately.]

Why, yes, on the whole I think you do.

CERINTHY.

Well! one thing I must say, — I can't see what *he* finds in me. I think he is a thousand times too good for me. Why, you have no idea, Mary, how I *have* plagued him. Besides, I have told him everything I could think of to discourage him. I told him that I had a bad temper and did n't believe the doctrines, and could n't promise that I ever should ; and after all, that creature keeps right on, and I don't know what to tell him.

MARY.

[mildly.]

Well, do you think you really love him ?

CERINTHY.

[giving a great flounce.]

Love him? to be sure I don't! Catch me loving any man! I told him last night I did n't, but it did n't do a bit of good. I used to think that man was bashful, but I declare I have altered my mind; he will talk and talk till I don't know what to do. I tell you, Mary, he talks beautifully too, sometimes.

[Here Cerinthy turns quickly away, and begins playing with Mary's scissors and thread. After a few moments she resumes.]

The fact is, Mary, that man *needs* somebody to take care of him; for he never thinks of himself. They say he has got the consumption; but he has n't, any more than I have. It is just the way he neglects himself, — preaching, talking, and visiting; nobody to take care of him and see to his clothes, and nurse him up when he gets a little hoarse and run down. I do know how to keep things in order; and if I should keep *such* a man's soul in his body, I should be doing some good in the world; because if ministers don't live, of course they can't convert anybody. Just think of his saying that I could be a comfort to *him!* I told him that it was perfectly ridiculous. "And besides," says I, "what will everybody think?" I thought that I had really talked him out of the notion of it last night; but there he was in again this morning, and told me he had derived great encouragement from what I had

said.   Well, the poor man really is lonesome, — his
mother's dead, and he hasn't any sisters.   I asked
him why he didn't go and take Miss Olladine
Slocum; everybody says she would make a first-
rate minister's wife.

MARY.

Well, and what did he say to that?

CERINTHY.

[looking down.]
  Well, something really silly, — about my looks.

MARY.

[looking up at Cerinthy.]
  Probably he is a man of taste, Cerinthy; I advise you to leave the matter entirely to his judgment.

CERINTHY.

You don't really, Mary!   Don't you think it
would injure *him*, if I should?

MARY.

I think not, materially.

CERINTHY.

[rising.]
  Well, the men will be coming home from the
mowing before I get home, and want their supper.
Mother has got one of her headaches on this after-

noon, so I can't stop any longer. There is n't a soul in the house knows where anything is when I am gone. If I should ever take it into my head to go off, I don't know what would become of father and mother.

MARY.

Does your mother know anything about it?

CERINTHY.

Oh, as to mother, I believe she has been hoping and praying about it these three months. She thinks I am such a desperate case, it is the only way I am to be brought in, as she calls it. That's what set me against him at first; but the fact is, if girls will let a man argue with them, he always contrives to get the best of it. I am kind of provoked about it too. But mercy on us! he is so meek, there is no use of getting provoked at him. Well, I guess I will go home and think about it.

Curtain falls.

THE ART OF BEDMAKING.

(IN ONE SCENE.)

———◆———

CHARACTERS.

MISS OPHELIA ST. CLARE.
EVA ST. CLARE, cousin to Miss Ophelia.
TOPSY, a little negress.
ROSA, a quadroon girl.

COSTUMES.

MISS OPHELIA. A plain full-skirted dress.
EVA. A short, white, full-skirted dress, and a coral necklace.
TOPSY. A printed cotton dress, clean, well-starched apron, and short hair.
ROSA. A neat but gay cotton dress. Apron and coral earrings.

ANALYSIS OF SCENE: PROPERTIES.

SCENE. A bedroom with exit. Miss Ophelia instructs Topsy in the art of bedmaking.
PROPERTIES. Table, chairs, bed, and bedclothes. Ribbon and gloves. Basket of clothes.

SCENE. *A bedroom.*

[Miss Ophelia takes Topsy into her chamber, and solemnly commences a course of instruction in the art and mystery of bedmaking. Behold, then, Topsy, washed and shorn of all the little braided tails wherein her soul delighted, arrayed in a clean gown with well-starched apron, standing reverently before Miss Ophelia, with an expression of solemnity well befitting a funeral.]

Curtain rises on Miss Ophelia and Topsy.

MISS OPHELIA.

Now, Topsy, I 'm going to show you just how my bed is to be made. I am very particular about my bed. You must learn exactly how to do it.

TOPSY.

[with a deep sigh and a face of woful earnestness.]
Yes, ma'am.

MISS OPHELIA.

Now, Topsy, look here : this is the hem of the sheet, this is the right side of the sheet, and this is the wrong ; will you remember ?

TOPSY.

[with another sigh.]
Yes, ma'am.

MISS OPHELIA.

Well now, the undersheet you must bring under the bolster, — so, — and tuck it clear down under the mattress, nice and smooth, — so ; — do you see ?

TOPSY.

[with profound attention.]
Yes, ma'am.

MISS OPHELIA.

But the upper sheet must be brought down in this way, and tucked under firm and smooth at the foot, — so, — the narrow hem at the foot.

TOPSY.

Yes, ma'am.

[Miss Ophelia does not see that, during the time when the good lady's back is turned, in the zeal of her manipulations, the young disciple has contrived to snatch a pair of gloves and a ribbon, which she has adroitly slipped into her sleeves, and stands with her hands dutifully folded as before.]

MISS OPHELIA.

[pulling off the clothes and seating herself.]

Now, Topsy, let's see *you* do this.

[Topsy with great gravity and adroitness goes through the exercise completely to Miss Ophelia's satisfaction, smoothing the sheets, patting out every wrinkle, and exhibiting through the whole process a gravity and seriousness with which her instructress is greatly edified. By an unlucky slip, however, a fluttering fragment of the ribbon hangs out of one of her sleeves, just as she is finishing, and catches Miss Ophelia's attention.]

MISS OPHELIA.

[pouncing upon the ribbon.]

What's this? You naughty, wicked child! — you've been stealing this!

[The ribbon is pulled out of Topsy's own sleeve, yet she is not in the least disconcerted ; she only looks at it with an air of the most surprised and unconscious innocence.]

TOPSY.

Laws! why, that 'ar 's Miss Feely's ribbon, ain't it? How could it a-got caught in my sleeve?

MISS OPHELIA.

Topsy, you naughty girl, don't you tell me a lie, — you stole that ribbon!

TOPSY.

Missis, I declare for 't I did n't; never see'd it till dis yer blessed minit.

MISS OPHELIA.

Oh, Topsy! Topsy! don't you know it 's wicked to tell lies?

TOPSY.

I never tells no lies, Miss Feely; it 's jist the truth I 've been a-telling now, and ain't nothin' else.

MISS OPHELIA.

Topsy, I shall have to whip you, if you tell lies so.

TOPSY.

[beginning to blubber.]

Laws, missis, if you 's to whip all day, could n't say no other way; I never see'd dat 'ar, — it must have got caught in my sleeve.

MISS OPHELIA.

[indignantly catching the child and shaking her.]

Don't you tell me that again !

[The shake brings the gloves on to the floor from the other sleeve.]

There, you ! will you tell me now you did n't steal the ribbon ?

TOPSY.

No, missis, I'se never touched the ribbon ! I did take them gloves, but I never see'd dat 'ar ribbon till dis yer minit.

MISS OPHELIA.

Now, Topsy, if you 'll confess all about it, I won't whip you this time.

TOPSY.

[with many sighs and tears.]

Laws ! Miss Feely, den, I did take 'em, but I 'll never do so no more.   I know I 'se wicked.

MISS OPHELIA.

Well, now, tell me, — I know you must have taken other things since you have been in the house.   Now tell me if you took anything, and I shan't whip you.

TOPSY.

Laws, missis !   I took Miss Eva's red thing, she wa'ars on her neck.

MISS OPHELIA.

You did? You naughty child! Well, what else?

TOPSY.

I took Rosa's yer-rings — them red ones.

MISS OPHELIA.

Go bring them to me this minute, both of 'em.

TOPSY.

Laws, missis! I can't — they 's burnt up!

MISS OPHELIA.

Burnt up! — what a story! Go get 'em, or I 'll whip you!

TOPSY.

[with tears and groans.]

I can't, Miss Feely, I can't! They 's burnt up, they is.

MISS OPHELIA.

What did you burn 'em for?

TOPSY.

'Cause I 'se wicked, I is. I 'se mighty wicked anyhow — I can't help it.

[Just at that moment little Eva comes into the room with the identical coral necklace on her neck.]

MISS OPHELIA.

Why, Eva! where did you get your necklace?

EVA.

Get it? Why, I had it on all day

MISS OPHELIA.

Did you have it on yesterday?

EVA.

Yes; and what is funny, aunty, I had it on all night. I forgot to take it off when I went to bed.

[Miss Ophelia looks perfectly bewildered, the more so, as Rosa, at that instant, comes into the room, with a basket of newly-ironed linen on her head, and the coral eardrops shaking in her ears.]

MISS OPHELIA.

[in despair.]

I 'm sure I can't tell what to do with such a child! What in the world did you tell me you took those things for, Topsy?

TOPSY.

Why, missis said I must 'fess; and I could n't think of nothin' else to 'fess.

MISS OPHELIA.

But, of course, I did n't want you to confess things you did n't do; that 's telling a lie, just as much as the other.

TOPSY.

[with an air of innocent wonder.]

Laws, now, is it ?

ROSA.

[looking indignantly at Topsy.]

La, there ain't any such thing as truth in that limb. If I was Mas'r St. Clare, I'd whip her till the blood run. I would — I'd let her catch it !

EVA.

[with an air of command.]

No, no, Rosa; you must n't talk so, Rosa; I can't bear to hear it.

ROSA.

La sakes ! Miss Eva, you's so good ; you don't know nothing how to get along with niggers. There's no way but to cut 'em well up, I tell ye.

EVA.

Rosa ! hush ! Don't say another word of that sort !

[Rosa is cowed in a moment and goes away. Eva stands looking at Topsy with a perplexed and sorrowful expression.]

Poor Topsy, why need you steal? You're going to be taken good care of now. I'm sure I'd rather give you anything of mine, than have you steal it.

Curtain falls.

THE POWER OF LOVE.

(IN ONE SCENE.)

———◆———

CHARACTERS.

AUGUSTINE ST. CLARE.

MISS OPHELIA ST. CLARE, cousin to Augustine.

EVA ST. CLARE, a little girl, daughter to Augustine.

TOPSY, a little negress, slave to Augustine St. Clare.

COSTUMES.

ST. CLARE. A cool and old-fashioned suit of clothes, such as was worn by gentlemen in the morning, about 1850.

MISS OPHELIA. A handsome, full-skirted dress, lace shawl, "coal-scuttle" straw bonnet, trimmed with ribbons, etc.

EVA. A white dress.

TOPSY. Bright cotton dress and white apron.

ANALYSIS OF SCENE: PROPERTIES.

SCENE. A parlor with exit. Miss Ophelia finds Topsy in mischief and declares she will trouble herself with her no longer. Eva tries to persuade her to be good.

PROPERTIES. Parlor furniture, mats, etc.

SCENE. *A parlor.*

Curtain rises on St. Clare and Eva.

[Eva comes at St. Clare's call, and sits on his knee. They soon hear loud exclamations from the next room and violent reproof addressed to somebody.]

MISS OPHELIA (*within*).

You naughty, wicked, wasteful child!

ST. CLARE.

What new witchcraft has Tops been brewing?
That commotion is of her raising, I 'll be bound.

[And in a moment after, Miss Ophelia, in high indignation,
comes dragging the culprit along.]

Enter Miss Ophelia with Topsy.

MISS OPHELIA.

Come out here, now! I *will* tell your master!

ST. CLARE.

What 's the case now?

MISS OPHELIA.

The case is, that I cannot be plagued with this
child any longer! It 's past all bearing; flesh and
blood cannot endure it. Here I locked her up and
gave her a hymn to study; and what does she do
but spy out where I put my key, and has gone to
my bureau, and got a bonnet trimming, and cut it
all to pieces to make dolls' jackets. I never saw
anything like it in my life! I 'm sure, Augustine, ¯
I don't know what to do. I 've taught and taught,
I 've talked till I 'm tired; I 've whipped her; I 've
punished her in every way I can think of, and still
she 's just what she was at first.

ST. CLARE.

[amused at the child's expression.]

Come here, Tops, you monkey! What makes you behave so?

TOPSY.

[demurely.]

'Spects it's my wicked heart; Miss Feely says so.

ST. CLARE.

Don't you see how much Miss Ophelia has done for you? She says she has done everything she can think of.

TOPSY.

Lor' yes, mas'r and old missis used to say so too. She whipped me a heap harder and used to pull my har and knock my head agin the door; but it did n't do me no good. I 'spects, if they 's to pull every spear o' har out o' my head, it would n't do no good, neither, I 's so wicked. Laws, I 's nothin' but a nigger, noways.

MISS OPHELIA.

Well, I shall have to give her up; I can't have that trouble any longer.

ST. CLARE.

[rising from his seat.]

Well, I 'd just like to ask one question.

MISS OPHELIA.

What is it ?

ST. CLARE.

Why, if your gospel is not strong enough to save one heathen child that you can have at home here all to yourself, what's the use of sending one or two poor missionaries off with it among thousands of just such? I suppose this child is about a fair sample of what thousands of your heathen are.

[Miss Ophelia does not make an immediate answer, and St. Clare leaves the room. His cousin follows him, a minute later, and the children are left alone.]

Exeunt St. Clare and Miss Ophelia.

EVA.

What does make you so bad, Topsy? Why won't you try and be good? Don't you love any-body, Topsy?

TOPSY.

Dunno nothing 'bout love; I loves candy and sich, that's all.

EVA.

But you love your father and mother?

TOPSY.

Never had none, ye know. I telled ye that, Miss Eva.

EVA.

[sadly.]

Oh, I know ; but had n't you any brother, or sister, or aunt, or —

TOPSY.

No, none on 'em ; never had nothing nor nobody.

EVA.

But, Topsy, if you 'd only try to be good, you might —

TOPSY.

Could n't never be nothin' but a nigger, if I was ever so good. If I could be skinned and come white, I 'd try then.

EVA.

But people can love you, if you are black, Topsy. Miss Ophelia would love you if you were good.

[Topsy gives a short blunt laugh, expressive of incredulity.]

Don't you think so ?

TOPSY.

[beginning to whistle.]

No, she can't bar me 'cause I 'm a nigger ! she 'd 's soon have a toad touch her ! There can't nobody love niggers, and niggers can't do nothin' ! *I* don't care !

EVA.

[with a sudden burst of feeling, and laying her little, thin, white hand on Topsy's shoulder.]

Oh, Topsy, poor child, *I* love you! I love you because you have n't any father, or mother, or friends, because you have been a poor abused child. I love you, and I want you to be good. It really grieves me to have you be so naughty. I wish you would try to be good for my sake.

[The round, keen eyes of the black child are overcast with tears ; large, bright drops roll heavily down, one by one, and fall on the little white hand. She lays her head down between her knees, and weeps and sobs, while the beautiful child bends over her.]

Poor Topsy! don't you know that Jesus loves all alike ? He is just as willing to love you as me. He loves you just as I do, only more because He is better. He will help you to be good ; and you can go to heaven at last, and be an angel forever, just as much as if you were white. Only think of it, Topsy! *You* can be one of those spirits bright, Uncle Tom sings about.

TOPSY.

Oh, dear Miss Eva, dear Miss Eva! I will try, I will try! I never did care nothin' about it before.

Curtain falls.

THE PRACTICAL TEST.

(IN ONE SCENE.)

CHARACTERS.

DR. HOPKINS, a minister.
MR. MARVYN.
MRS. MARVYN, his wife.
CANDACE, a negress and slave to Mr. Marvyn.

COSTUMES.

DR. HOPKINS. Full coat and small-clothes of broadcloth, black silk stockings, shoes with buckles. Cocked hat, full-bottomed wig. " White wrist ruffles " and " plaited shirt-bosom."

MR. MARVYN. Plain but neat coat and small-clothes.

MRS. MARVYN. Full stuff skirt and white " short-gown." Cap and apron.

CANDACE. Linsey petticoat and bodice, clean white apron, and red and yellow turban, arranged " so as to give to her head the air of an immense butterfly."

ANALYSIS OF SCENE: PROPERTIES.

SCENE. A parlor with exit. Dr. Hopkins proposes to Mr. Marvyn to offer freedom to his slaves.

PROPERTIES. Furniture, mats, etc., suitable for a sitting-room.

Scene. *A parlor.*

Curtain rises on Mr. and Mrs. Marvyn and Dr. Hopkins.

DR. HOPKINS.

My mind labors with this subject of the enslaving of the Africans, Mr. Marvyn. We have just been declaring to the world that all men are born with an inalienable right to liberty. We have fought for it, and the Lord of Hosts has been with us; and can we stand before Him with our foot upon our brother's neck?

MR. MARVYN.

[Mr. Marvyn's face flushes, his eye kindles, and his compressed respiration shows how deeply the subject moves him. Mrs. Marvyn's eyes cast on him a look of anxious inquiry.]

Doctor, I have thought of the subject myself. Mrs. Marvyn has lately been reading a pamphlet of Mr. Thomas Clarkson's, on the slave trade, and she was saying to me only last night, that she did not see but the argument extended equally to holding slaves. One thing, I confess, stumbles me: Was there not an express permission given to Israel to buy and hold slaves of old?

DR. HOPKINS.

Doubtless; but many permissions were given to them which were local and temporary, for if we hold them to apply to the human race, the Turks might quote the Bible for making slaves of us, if they could, — and the Algerines have the Scripture all on their side, — and our own blacks, at some future time, if they can get the power, might justify themselves in making slaves of us.

MR. MARVYN.

I assure you, sir, if I speak, it is not to excuse myself. But I am quite sure my servants do not desire liberty, and would not take it if it were offered.

DR. HOPKINS.

Call them in and try it. If they refuse, it is their own matter.

MR. MARVYN.

[calmly.]

Cato is up at the light-acre lot, but you may call in Candace. My dear, call Candace, and let the Doctor put the question to her.

Exit Mrs. Marvyn, reëntering in a minute or two followed by Candace.

[Candace sinks a dutiful curtsy, and stands twirling her thumbs, while the Doctor surveys her gravely.]

DR. HOPKINS.

Candace, do you think it right that the black race should be slaves to the white ?

[The face and air of Candace present a curious picture at this moment ; a sort of rude sense of delicacy embarrasses her, and she turns a deprecating look, first on Mrs. Marvyn and then on her master.]

MR. MARVYN.

Don't mind us, Candace ; tell the Doctor the exact truth.

CANDACE.

[After a moment's pause, her immense person heaving with her labored breathing.]

Ef I must speak, I must. No, — I neber did tink 't was right. When Gineral Washington was here, I hearn 'em read de Declaration ob Independence and Bill o' Rights ; an' I tole Cato den, says I, " Ef dat ar' true, you an' I are as free as anybody." It stands to reason. Why, look at me, — I ain't a critter. I 's neider huffs nor horns. I 's a reasonable bein' — a woman — as much a woman as anybody.

[holding up her head with an air as majestic as a palm-tree.]

An' Cato, he 's a man born free an' equal, ef dar 's any truth in what you read. Dat 's all.

MR. MARVYN.

But, Candace, you 've always been contented and happy with us, have you not?

CANDACE.

Yes, Mass'r, — I ha'n't got nuffin to complain ob in dat matter. I could n't hab no better friends 'n you an' Missis.

MR. MARVYN.

Would you like your liberty, if you could get it, though? Answer me honestly.

CANDACE.

Why, to be sure I should! Who would n't? Mind ye,

[earnestly raising her black, heavy hand.]

ta' on't dat I want to go off, or want to shirk work; but I want to *feel free.* Dem dat is n't free has nuffin to gib to nobody; — dey can't show what dey would do.

MR. MARVYN.

[solemnly.]

Well, Candace, from this day you are free.

[Candace covers her face with both her fat hands, and shakes and trembles, and finally, throwing her apron over her head, makes a desperate rush for the door, and throws herself down in the kitchen in a perfect torrent of tears and sobs.]

Exit Candace.

DR. HOPKINS.

You see what freedom is to every human creature. The blessing of the Lord will be upon this deed, Mr. Marvyn. " The steps of a just man are ordered by the Lord, and he delighteth in his way."

Reënter Candace.

[her butterfly turban somewhat deranged with the violence of her prostration.]

CANDACE.

[with a clearing-up snuff.]

I want ye all to know, dat it 's my will an' pleasure to go right on doin' my work jes' de same; an',

Missis, please, I 'll allers put three eggs in de crullers, now; an' I won't turn de wash-basin down in de sink, but hang it jam-up on de nail; an' I won't pick up chips in a milkpan, ef I 'm in ever so big a hurry; — I 'll do eberyting jes' as ye tells me. Now you try me an' see ef I won't.

MR. MARVYN.

I intend to make the same offer to your husband, when he returns from work to-night.

CANDACE.

Laws, Mass'r, — why, Cato, he 'll do jes' as I do, — dere ain't no kind o' need o' askin' him. Course he will!

Curtain falls.

THE VILLAGE DO-NOTHING.

———◆———

CHARACTERS.

SAM LAWSON, the "do-nothing," "a tall, shambling, loose-jointed" man.

AUNT LOIS.

COSTUMES.

SAM LAWSON, in loose, shabby, untidy clothes.

AUNT LOIS, a stuff petticoat and printed cotton "short-gown," and apron.

ANALYSIS OF SCENE: PROPERTIES.

SCENE. A kitchen with exit. Sam Lawson comes to mend the clock, and is reproved by Aunt Lois for his dilatoriness.

PROPERTIES. Plain chairs, and other kitchen furniture. Table with clock-weights, wheels, etc. upon it.

SCENE. *A kitchen.*

Curtain rises on Aunt Lois and Sam Lawson smoking.

SAM LAWSON.

Why, ye see, Miss Lois, clocks can't be druv; that's jest what they can't. Some things can be druv, and then again some things can't, and clocks is that kind. They's jest got to be humored.

Now this 'ere's a 'mazin' good clock; give me my time on it, and I'll have it so 't will keep straight on to the Millennium.

AUNT LOIS.

[with a snort of infinite contempt.]
Millennium!

SAM LAWSON.

[letting fall his work in a contemplative manner.]

Yes, the Millennium : that 'ere's an interestin' topic. Now Parson Lothrop, he don't think the Millennium will last a thousand years. What's your 'pinion on that pint, Miss Lois?

AUNT LOIS.

[in her most nipping tones.]

My opinion is, that if folks don't mind their own business, and do with their might what their hand finds to do, the Millennium won't come at all.

SAM LAWSON.

Wal, you see, Miss Lois, it's just here : — one day is with the Lord as a thousand years, and a thousand years as one day.

AUNT LOIS.

I should think you thought a day was a thousand years, the way you work.

[sitting down with his back to his desperate litter of wheels, weights, and pendulums, and meditatively caressing his knee as he watches the sailing clouds in abstract meditation.]

Wal, ye see, ef a thing 's ordained, why it 's got to be, ef you don't lift a finger. That 'ere's *so* now, ain't it?

Sam Lawson, you are about the most aggravating creature I ever had to do with. Here you 've got our clock all to pieces, and have been keeping up a perfect hurrah's nest in our kitchen for three days, and there you sit maundering and talking with your back to your work, fussing about the Millennium, which is none of your business, or mine, as I know of! Do either put that clock together or let it alone!

Don't you be a grain uneasy, Miss Lois! Why, I 'll have your clock all right in the end, but I can't be druv. Wal, I guess I 'll take another spell on 't to-morrow or Friday.

[horror-stricken, but seeing herself actually in the hands of the imperturbable enemy, now essays the task of conciliation.]

Now do, Lawson, just finish up this job, and I 'll pay you down, right on the spot; and you need the money.

SAM LAWSON.

I 'd like to 'blige you, Miss Lois; but ye see money ain't everything in this world. Ef I work tew long on one thing, my mind kind o' gives out, ye see ; and besides, I 've got some 'sponsibilities to 'tend to. There 's Mrs. Captain Brown, she made me promise to come to-day and look at the nose o' that 'ere silver teapot o' hern ; it 's kind o' sprung a leak. And then I 'greed to split a little oven-wood for the Widdah Pedee, that lives up on the Shelburn road. Must visit the widdahs in their affliction, Scriptur' says. And then there 's Hepsy : she 's allers a-castin' it up at me that I don't do nothing for her and the chil'en ; but then, lordy massy, Hepsy hain't no kind o' patience. Why jest this mornin' I was a-tellin' her to count up her marcies, and I 'clare for 't if I did n't think she 'd 'a' throwed the tongs at me. That 'ere woman's temper railly makes me consarned. Wal, good day, Miss Lois, I 'll be along again to-morrow or Friday or the first o' next week.

Exit Sam singing.

Thy years are an
Etarnal day,
Thy years are an
Etarnal day.

AUNT LOIS.

[with a snap.]

An Eternal torment! I 'm sure, if there 's a mortal creature on this earth that I pity, it 's Hepsy

Lawson. Folks talk about her scolding. That Sam Lawson is enough to make the saints in heaven fall from grace. And you can't *do* anything with him; it 's like charging bayonet into a woolsack.

Curtain falls on Aunt Lois.

SAM LAWSON'S THANKSGIVING DINNER.

(IN ONE SCENE.)

CHARACTERS.

SAM LAWSON.
MRS. BADGER.
MISS LOIS, her daughter.
HORACE and HARRY, two little boys.

COSTUMES.

SAM LAWSON. A loose, untidy suit of clothes.
MRS. BADGER. A plain skirt and bodice of dark stuff, white cap, apron and handkerchief, pinned round her neck.
MISS LOIS. Stuff skirt, cotton "short-gown," and apron.
The boys. Knickerbockers and blouses, belted round the waist.

ANALYSIS OF SCENE: PROPERTIES.

SCENE. Kitchen with exit. Mrs. Badger rebukes Sam for his idleness and gives him a turkey.
PROPERTIES. Plain furniture, a turkey, and two pies. Also apples, raisins, etc.

SCENE. *A kitchen.*

Curtain rises on Mrs. Badger, Miss Lois, Harry and Horace, chopping mince-meat, paring apples, etc.

MISS LOIS.

There, to be sure, — there comes Sam Lawson down the hill, limpsy as ever. Now he'll have his doleful story to tell, and mother 'll give him one of the turkeys.

Enter Sam Lawson.

[Sam comes in with his usual air of plaintive assurance, and seats himself a contemplative spectator in the chimney-corner, regardless of the looks and signs of unwelcome on the part of Aunt Lois.]

SAM LAWSON.

[in musing tones.]

Lordy massy, how prosperous everything does seem here ! so different from what 't is t' our house. There's Hepsy, she 's all in a stew, an' I 've just been an' got her thirty-seven cents wuth o' nutmegs, yet she says she 's sure she don't see how she 's to keep Thanksgiving, an' she 's down on me about it, jest as ef 't was my fault. Yeh see, last winter our old gobbler got froze. You know, Mis' Badger, that 'ere cold night we hed last winter. Wal, I was off with Jake Marshall that night. Ye see, Jake, he hed to take old General Dearborn's corpse into Boston to the family vault, and Jake he kind o' hated to go alone, 't was a drefful cold time, and he ses to me, "Sam, you jes' go 'long with me ; " so I was sort o' sorry for him, and I kind o' thought I 'd go 'long. Wal, come 'long to Josh Bissel's tahvern, there at the Halfway House, you know, 't was so swinging cold we stopped to take a little suthin' warmin', an' we sort o' sot an' sot over the fire, till, fust we knew, we kind o' got asleep ; an' when we woke up we found we 'd left the old

General hitched up t' th' post pretty much all night. Wal, did n't hurt him none, poor man ; 't was allers a favorite spot o' his'n. But takin' one thing with another, I did n't get home till about noon next day, an', I tell you, Hepsy she was right down on me. She said the baby was sick, and there had n't been no wood split, nor the barn fastened up, nor nothin'. Lordy massy, I did n't mean no harm ; I thought there was wood enough, and I thought likely Hepsy 'd git out an' fasten up the barn. But Hepsy, she was in one o' her contrary streaks, an' she would n't do a thing ; an' when I went out to look, why, sure 'nuff, there was our old tom-turkey froze as stiff as a stake, — his claws jest a-stickin' right straight up like this.

[Here Sam strikes an expressive attitude, and looks so much like a frozen turkey as to give a pathetic reality to the picture.]

MRS. BADGER.

Well now, Sam, why need you be off on things that 's none of your business? I 've talked to you plainly about that a great many times, Sam.

[continuing in tones of severe admonition.]

Hepsy is a hard-working woman, but she cannot be expected to see to everything, and you oughter have been at home that night to fasten up your own barn and look after your own creeturs.

[Sam takes the rebuke all the more meekly as he perceives the stiff black legs of a turkey poking out from under my grandmother's apron, while she is delivering it.]

See now, Sam, take these to Hepsy, and the children.

[giving him the turkey and taking two pies from the table.] Poor things! they ought to have something good to eat Thanksgiving day; 't ain't their fault that they 've got a shiftless father. Here, boys, you carry these pies down to Hepsy!

[giving one to each boy.]

SAM LAWSON.

Thanks, Mis' Badger. A body 'd think that Hepsy 'd learn to trust in Providence, but she don't. She allers hes a Thanksgiving dinner pervided; but that 'ere woman ain't grateful for it, by no manner o' means. Now she 'll be jest as cross as she can be, 'cause this 'ere ain't *our* turkey, and these 'ere ain't *our* pies. Folks does lose so much that hes sech dispositions.

Exit Sam, followed by the two boys carrying the pies.

Curtain falls.

www.ingramcontent.com/pod-product-compliance
Lightning Source LLC
Chambersburg PA
CBHW020026030726
47499CB00007B/2296